S0-BOB-172

HANDY-DANDY
HELPFUL HAL

A BOOK ABOUT
HELPFULNESS

Michael P. Waite
Illustrated by Gary Trousdale

Chariot Books
DAVID C.COOK PUBLISHING CO.

To my Grandfather, Clyde Waite, who
taught me all about politics, eating right, and
the importance of pleasant yesterdays. *MPW*

To the helpful and influential people, silly
and sensible alike. *GAT*

Chariot Books is an imprint of David C. Cook Publishing Co.
David C. Cook Publishing Co., Elgin, Illinois 60120
David C. Cook Publishing Co., Weston, Ontario
HANDY-DANDY HELPFUL HAL
© 1987 by Michael P. Waite for text and illustrations

All rights reserved. Except for brief excerpts for review purposes, no part of this book may be reproduced or used in any form
without written permission from the publisher.

Cover design by Dawn Lauck
First printing, 1987
Printed in the United States of America

95 94 93   15 14 13 12 11 10 9
Library of Congress Cataloging-in-Publication Data
Waite, Michael P., 1960-
    Handy-Dandy Helpful Hal.
    (Building Christian character series)
    Summary: Helpful Hal shows Sam and Sue the importance of helping theirparents by doing chores such as hanging up
clothes, washing the car, and feeding the cat.
    [1. Helpfulness—Fiction. 2. Family life—Fiction. 3. Christian life—Fiction. 4. Stories in rhyme] I. Trousdale, Gary, ill. II.
Title. III. Series: Waite, Michael P., 1960-   . Building Christian character series.
PZ8.3.W136Han 1987   [E]   87-5275
ISBN 1-55513-221-9

There we were, in our backyard,
My wife and I were working hard.
We had a giant list of chores . . .
To be exact, nine-thousand-four!

Both our children, Sam and Sue,
Told us they had things to do . . .
Like sipping slushy lemonade
On the hammock, in the shade!

5

As I wiped my sweaty brow,
And rested on my rusty plow,
A funny fellow came my way.
He crossed my lawn and said, "Good day!"

He pulled a wagon full of things—
Like tools and mops and paints and strings.
That man had gadgets everywhere—
Inside his boots, up to his hair!

He came right up and shook my hand,
"Aha!" he said, "You're just the man!
I'm Handy-Dandy Helpful Hal,
The Pooped-Out Parents' Perfect Pal!"

Hal went up to Sam and Sue
And whispered in their ears, "Yoooo Hoooo!
Up and at 'em, sleepy heads,
Mom and Pop are pooped," he said.
"Time for you to lend a hand,
Better help them while you can!"

"With all this lying 'round like slugs
I'm sure you'll both turn into Gluggs.
I'm sure you've heard of Gluggs before?
All they do is eat and snore—
Giant things, all green and chubby. . . .
Say there, Sam, you're getting tubby."

Next thing I knew my feet were draggin'
Off the back of Hal's big wagon. . . .

Through the door with one quick pounce,
And up the stairs without a bounce.

13

He rolled us into Sammy's room
And handed Sam a purple broom.
"Time to clean your room," he said,
"Do you know how to make a bed?
These are chores a kid can do. . . .
I've cleaned my room since I was two."

My wife and I were quite surprised—
The kids cleaned up before our eyes!

No sooner had they finished that
Than Hal called in the dog and cat.

"I think these pets are yours," he said.
"Every day they must be fed.
A simple chore, I think you'll find,
Let's try it once, if you don't mind!"

16

Sam and Sue each filled a dish
With Puppy Pork and Frisky Fish.
They filled the other bowls with water.
Could this be MY son and daughter?

"Good!" said Hal and off we went
Like a hound dog on a scent.
At the kitchen sink he stopped
And said, "I'll need you, Mom and Pop!"

"These kids can wash the pots and pans,
But they have tiny little hands,
And so it's best if everyone
Joins in to get the dishes done!"

19

Before we knew what Hal was saying
Soap was sudsing, water spraying.
Soon we had those dishes clean—
Washed and dried just like a dream!

"While we're here," said Helpful Hal,
"Shall we do more? I think we shall!
Here we have the kitchen trash,
You can dump it in a flash!
Just put it in a plastic bag,
And out you go . . . don't let it drag!"

21

"Very nicely done!" said Hal.
"I told you I'm a parents' pal!
Now off we go! Out to the yard!
I'll bet these kids can wash a car!"

22

"Here's a chore we all can do,"
Said Hal, and then the water flew.
"I've washed at least a million cars,
I've washed the cars of Movie Stars!
And if, perhaps, you think I'm fibbin'
Here's my First—Place Washer's Ribbon!"

23

Susie hosed while Sammy scrubbed,
We soaped and washed and wiped and rubbed,

And soon that car was shiny bright.
"Good job!" said Hal. "You've done all right."

24

"Now quickly, let's complete our chores,
We'll pull some weeds since we're outdoors—
Be sure you check with Mom or Pop
So you don't yank a carrot top!"

"Last of all, let's get the rake
And pile these leaves, for goodness sake!
And when we've made a giant heap,
It's lots of fun to take a leap!"

"There!" said Hal. "I think we're done!
Wasn't that a lot of fun?
You were splendid, Sam and Sue—
See the things that you can do?"

"When you help your mom and dad
The chores don't really seem so bad.
And everything gets done so soon,
That you still have the afternoon!"

"Why not travel to the ocean?
Don't forget your suntan lotion!
How about a camping trip?
Go to the pool and take a dip!
A game of tennis? Maybe two?
When did you last see the zoo?"

28

"Thank you, Helpful Hal," I said.
"You've taught our kids to make their beds,
You showed them how to feed the cat,
And how to wash the car in fact!
You showed them how to fold their clothes,
And on and on your helping goes."

"But now that we have done our chores,
There's something else to do outdoors—
Swimming, zoos, and mountain hikes
Aren't the sort of things we like.
I hope that you won't think us rude,
But we have quite another mood!"

And with those words, my wife and I
Took our children at our side
And crawled up on the hammock swing
To do our very favorite thing!